TERRY DE...................ES

MUMMIES AND MAYHEM

Illustrated by Helen Flook

A & C BLACK
AN IMPRINT OF BLOOMSBURY
LONDON   NEW DELHI   NEW YORK   SYDNEY

First published by
A & C Black, an imprint of Bloomsbury Publishing plc
50 Bedford Square
London WC1B 3DP

www.bloomsbury.com

ISBN 978-1-4729-0669-4

A CIP catalogue for this book is available from the British Library.

Printed and Bound by CPI Group (UK) Ltd, Croydon CR0 4YY

1 3 5 7 9 10 8 6 4 2

THE **GOLD** IN THE **GRAVE**

Illustrated by Helen Flook

A & C BLACK
AN IMPRINT OF BLOOMSBURY
LONDON NEW DELHI NEW YORK SYDNEY

Chapter 1

The Perfect Plot

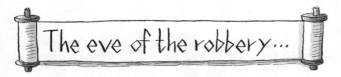

The water clock dripped. It was the
second hour of the afternoon and time
to go. Time to carry out the greatest
robbery in the history of the world.

There were four of us in the room. Four grave robbers. And we had the perfect plot.

They had been burying kings in Egypt for thousands of years. Burying them with gold and jewels to spend in the Afterlife.

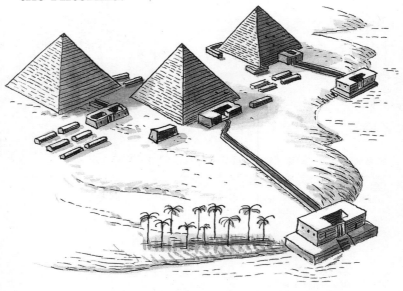

And people had been robbing those kings for thousands of years, to spend the fortunes in *this* life. Kings were buried in pyramids to guard their gold.

It didn't work.

No one used pyramids any more. They were too easy to rob. Now the kings were buried in tombs. Deep in the rocky cliffs near Thebes. There was only one way in – and that was guarded.

Dalifa was the temple jeweller who made ornaments for King Tutankhamen's tomb.

Antef was the master thief, the greatest tomb robber in the world.

"I have saved a lot of money," he said. "Now I am going to risk it all to win the biggest prize of all. And you are going to help me." He chuckled and showed his black and yellow stumps of teeth.

At least that was the idea. If we could rob the tomb of King Tutankhamen then we would be rich as kings. If we failed then our punishment would be horrible – so horrible it gave me nightmares.

Big Kerpes would be one of the coffin carriers at the sunset funeral of Tutankhamen.

Tutankhamen had been dead for seventy days. Days spent in turning his holy body into a mummy. From the first day of the King's death, Antef had been plotting the perfect plot.

Kerpes told me, "If they catch you they'll cut off your nose." He rubbed his own flat, broken nose. "If you are lucky."

"And if I am unlucky?" I asked.

"Then the new King Ay will have you crucified – nailed to the walls of Thebes city. He will show the world what happens to grave robbers."

"I don't want to be nailed to the wall, Kerpes," I whispered.

"Then don't get caught," he grunted.

Me? I am Paneb. In those days I was the poor son of a tavern owner. I wasn't very clever and I wasn't very brave. But I was very, very skinny. And that's why they wanted me.

Seventy days ago....

Antef had come to me in my father's
tavern where I was gathering pots. He
knew I was a thief. I would steal anything
– from washing on the riverbank where
it was stretched out to dry, to food in the
temple laid out for the gods.

"The plan is simple but brilliant," he told me. "The King's tomb is waiting for him in an underground cave across the river. He will be buried there with his fortune in seventy days time."

"And guarded," I said. "We can't get in."

He gave his gap-toothed grin again. "We don't have to. We just have to get *out*!"

"Uh?"

"The King will be placed in the tomb then the door will be sealed. But *you* will already be in there. On the inside. Hiding," he said. "We'll slip you in before the funeral."

I shuddered. "I'll be trapped in the tomb – in the dark – with the dead King and all the spirits? The door is a huge slab of stone. I won't be able to break out. I'll die."

He shook his head. "I have friends in the stone quarry. They have made the door. One corner has been cracked and put back with weak mortar. You can't see the fault unless you know it is there. You smash open the corner and pass out the King's fortune."

It was a clever plan. "How do I get in?"

"You go to the scribe school by the temple. The scribe master is a friend of mine. He will train you as a scribe, and you will be sent into the tomb to paint the prayers on the walls. The guards will get used to seeing you," he promised.

"So, after the funeral, I have to pass the treasure out through the corner of the door. You'll be waiting in the passage?" I asked.

"Yes."

"But the passage will be guarded," I argued. "If you can't get down to the door I'll be trapped alone."

"I have used most of my money to pay the guards," he said. "They will look the other way. And you will not be alone. Dalifa will be with you."

I looked at the girl who sat quietly chewing a date. She was dressed as a priestess.

My partner in crime.

Chapter 2

The Temple Trick

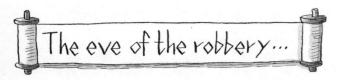

The eve of the robbery...

Antef smiled across at Dalifa and asked her, "How did you get on in the temple?"

Dalifa looked sour. "I had to wear a lot of uncomfortable clothes and do some disgusting things," she said. "I mean to say, I get my meat from a butcher in the market ... when I can afford it."

We nodded. I usually ate bread and onions but I had tasted meat. When I was rich – after the robbery – I would eat meat every day.

"But I've never had to kill my own meat!" Dalifa said.

"The priests made you kill something before you could eat it?" I asked.

She turned her narrow eyes on me with scorn. "You are as stupid as Kerpes," she snarled. "Every day they sacrifice a kid goat to the god Osiris. They gave me a live goat and told me to cut its throat, collect the blood in a bowl and cook the rest."

"Did you do it?" I asked.

"I did not," she said. "I took the goat to the butcher and swapped it for a bowl of blood and some cooked goat meat. The priests never knew."

"Did Osiris drink the blood?" I wanted to know.

Dalifa clenched her hands. "Osiris … is … a … stone … statue, Paneb. They make sacrifices to him and the peasants think Osiris drinks the blood, but he doesn't."

"So, who eats the cooked meat?" I asked.

Dalifa spread her hands. "The priests, of course! They have it for their evening meal."

"Poor Osiris must get hungry," I said.

"He … is … a … stone … oh, never mind!" Dalifa snapped.

Then she realised I was teasing and gave me a look as bitter as cobra venom.

"But the plot," Antef reminded her. "Did you get a job in the funeral of King Tutankhamen?"

Dalifa nodded once. "I travel with the funeral all the way. From the temple, over the river and all the way to the tomb."

"Ahh!" Antef breathed. "That is another piece of the plot in place."

"Then I hope I never have to go back to that blood-soaked temple again," Dalifa said. "The chief priest of Osiris is a terrifying man – and this morning he reminded us all of the hideous punishments we would suffer if there is a theft at the funeral."

Even Antef looked worried. But not as worried as when a shadow blocked the light from the doorway and a soldier stood there.

Chapter 3

The Grim Guard

The eve of the robbery...

The soldier was even larger than Kerpes. His face was scarred from battle blows and his voice was harsh as a vulture's cry.

"Antef – grave robber. I want a word with you and your friends."

"We've done nothing!" Antef said quickly.

"Tutankhamen's widow has sent me to check on all the grave robbers of Thebes. So what are you plotting?" the soldier asked.

Antef shrugged. "The boy was just showing us how the walls of the tomb are painted," he said.

"So show me," the soldier said and he knelt beside me.

The soldier picked up my sketch. I hadn't had time to hide it. "This looks like a plan of the King's tomb, Antef," he said.

"Really!" The old man gasped. "You surprise me, soldier."

The man clutched at his knife and straightened. "I am Khammale and I am not a simple soldier. I am captain of the palace guard."

"Sorry, officer," Antef smiled.

"I saw that idle Kerpes leave here a few moments ago. What part is he in the plot?" Khammale asked. "Coffin carrier?"

Antef tried to answer but, if he was like me, his mouth was too dry to speak. Dry with fear because Captain Khammale had already guessed that part of our plot.

He went on, "And I suppose the boy is a scribe who went in to the tomb to spy out the plan? The girl here will be a priestess, I expect."

"No!" Dalifa said. "I made some of the ornaments that will be going in the tomb."

"Shut up, Dalifa!" Antef said savagely. "The good officer doesn't want to know about that!"

"Oh, but I do," Captain Khammale said.

Dalifa smiled and said, "I've always made ornaments and little statues. So, of course, I was happy to offer my skills to the priests to make ornaments for Tutankhamen's tomb."

Captain Khammale nodded. "Now you will help Antef to take them out again. Melt the gold and silver down and make new ones to sell and make your fortune!"

"No!" Antef said. "We would never rob the grave of our dear, dead King. Never!"

"Good," Captain Khammale grinned. "Because if you try it, and if I catch you, I will tie you to a tree, then I will cut off your ears and then your nose. Then I will cut off little strips of skin one at a time and pour salt water into the cuts. Then I will let the ants and the jackals finish you off."

"Would you like that, Antef?"

The old man shook his head. My own mouth felt as dry as dust at the horror of the thought. The Captain rose and left.

"We can't go ahead now," I said.

Antef looked at the empty doorway. "Oh, yes we can, Paneb. I have spent all my money on this plot. There is no turning back now."

In the warm room I shivered.

Chapter 4

The Terrible Trap

"Antef," I snivelled, "I don't want to have my ears cut off! I'd scream!"

Dalifa threw her head back and laughed. "If your ears were cut off you wouldn't hear yourself!"

"It's not funny," I shouted.

The old man reached across, grabbed my tunic and hissed, "Captain Khammale was just guessing. He knows nothing. Anyway, he is just one man. He can't stop us."

Dalifa scoffed, "Paneb's frightened."

"You will have Dalifa with you. Think of the riches waiting for you," Antef breathed.

Dalifa smiled at me and said, "I have seen those riches, Paneb," she said proudly. "One golden servant for each day of the year and enough jewellery to break a camel's back," she went on.

"Kerpes and I will be waiting at the end of the tunnel with some strong men to carry it all to the boat." Antef added.

I blinked. "Tunnel? What tunnel? It's just a door into a passage. I pass the goods through a door."

"The King will be placed in his coffins – he has three of them," Antef explained. "Then the priests will sweep the floor and leave. They will close the door to the tomb and seal it. The King's workers will fill in the passage with stones to block it off."

"I'll be sealed behind a stone door and a passage full of stones? I can't dig my way out!" I argued.

"We will dig our way in," Antef said. That is why we have the stupid, but strong, Kerpes."

"I don't want to be shut in a tomb!" I wailed.

"It will only be for the night," Antef said. "We'll start digging a tunnel as soon as the workmen leave. We will pay the guards to look the other way. You'll be out as the sun rises."

"We'll take the treasures in a boat down the river. There are traders there waiting to buy them from us," Dalifa said.

"Just one day from now you will have more riches than you could earn in your lifetime as a peasant farmer."

"It's not the day I'm worried about. It's the night," I told them.

Antef laughed. He gripped my arm in his claw hand. "Time to take the boat," he said.

We stepped into the quiet streets.

"Everyone has gone to see the procession," Dalifa said, nodding towards the temple. "Time for me to join it." Dalifa waved goodbye.

Antef and I hurried down to the riverside where the huge barges were waiting to take Tutankhamen on his last voyage.

I just hoped it wouldn't be my last voyage too.

Chapter 5

To the Tomb

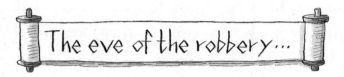

The eve of the robbery...

We slid over the water faster than a
fish and landed on the western shore.
The west where the sun set and where
Tutankhamen's spirit would soon be
travelling ... without his treasure.

The evening sun was cool as we crossed the desert. This was the road I'd taken every day for seventy days to Tutankhamen's tomb. I knew the way. But usually I walked with the other young scribes and our masters and a few of the royal archers.

Desert lions and jackals never troubled us and the archers would drive them off if they did.

But this evening Antef and I were alone and the cries of the creatures made our feet shuffle along the road as fast as our racing heartbeats.

Great piles of gravel stood by the entrance to the tomb. "That is ready to shovel in once the King is inside," Antef said.

"And me – they'll block me in too."

"Not for long," Antef said with a wink. "These stone workers are friends of mine. They will not fill it to the roof. We'll have you out in a couple of hours." He waved to one of the labourers who leaned on his shovel.

A guard blocked the door. He was there every day and he knew my face. That's what Antef had been hoping for. "The boy has come to finish the painting," the old man explained.

"A bit late," the guard grumbled. He looked across the desert to a cloud of dust that was rolling in from the river. The funeral parade. "They're almost here."

Antef turned on me and acted angry. "See, stupid boy? I told you this should have been finished yesterday." He slapped me with a horny hand and drove me into the corridor. "These boys are a waste of time!" he called as he passed the guard.

Servants and priests and craftsmen and scribes were in the tomb putting everything in its place, ready to receive the King.

I knew the room where Antef wanted me to hide. We passed through the entrance chamber where a golden chariot was lying in pieces on the floor. The King's servants would have to put it together to drive him into the Afterlife.

The light from the oil lamps glittered on all that gold. Gold everywhere, above my head and beneath my feet. I was dazzled by gold and my greed made me almost faint.

I slipped through the door into the back chamber that was packed with treasure and Antef began to close it behind me. "When the funeral arrives stay silent," he warned.

The door closed with a thud that sounded as hollow as my lonely heart felt.

The night of the robbery...

It was cool in the chamber, not cold. But I shivered. Gods and ghosts were haunting me. I swear they were there in the shadows.

I heard the workmen finish in the vault outside. Then a lot of noise as the funeral procession arrived and the priests placed the King in his coffins.

Then I heard a softer sound nearby as the door to my hiding place slid open. I crouched behind a large model boat. And waited for the thrust of a guard's sword. Instead I heard the hiss, "Paneb? Are you there?"

It was Dalifa. She closed the door quickly and gave me her sharp-eyed look. She whispered. "The funeral is over. They'll be sealing the tomb ... listen!"

I strained my ears. Suddenly the door swung open and lamplight spilled in. A guard stuck his head around the door and looked at us. I groaned. Nailed to the walls of Thebes, I knew it. I knew it would all go wrong.

The guard raised his lamp and grinned. "Are you all right, kids?" he asked.

"Kerpes?"

Dalifa hissed, "Go away baboon-brain."

The big man frowned. "Sorry. Just thought I'd see if you were comfortable."

"We'll all be comfortable nailed to the walls of Thebes," she spat. "Get out!"

"See you in the morning," the flat-nosed man said and closed the door. His footsteps clumped away.

After a while it was silent – silent as a grave! Dalifa gave a sharp nod. "Right, we are shut in. Start opening boxes and filling these pouches."

She lit an oil lamp and handed me some linen bags and began to fill them with golden arm bands and statues, jewels and rings.

I scrabbled in the wooden cases and came up with more. We moved out into the entry chamber and then into the burial room itself. Soon we had twenty bags filled with treasures.

Dalifa turned to the door and began to scrape at a crack in the top corner with her dagger. The corner broke off as Antef meant it to and there was just enough room for someone small like me or Dalifa to crawl through. But the far side was already blocked with small stones and they fell in on our heads.

"What if Antef doesn't come back for us?" I asked.

Dalifa pointed at the treasure. "For this Antef will chew his way through the stone. Be patient!"

And so we waited through the long night. Slowly I slipped into sleep. I awoke when stones fell through the broken corner of the door and Antef's face stared through.

"Time to go!" he said.

Chapter 6

The Face of Death

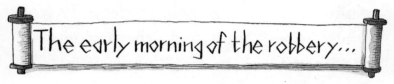

The early morning of the robbery...

I passed one of the bags to Antef and then helped Dalifa up to the opening. I crawled after her, clutching a bag full of rings. I stuffed it into my belt so I could use my hands to pull myself along.

Sharp stones scraped at my knees and elbows and the dust choked my throat and stung my eyes.

At last I felt the cool morning air on my face and blinked into the sunlight. Big Kerpes stood there, filthy from the digging but looking pleased. Antef was staring into his treasure bag, eyes alight with the morning sun.

Dalifa stretched out a hand for my treasure. I put my hand to my belt. The bag of rings had gone. It had fallen from my belt as I'd crawled along. We needed to make a few journeys. I'd find it later, I thought.

Then I looked up to the bank over the top of the entrance passage. A woman stood there. She wore a plain white gown and a rich wig. Her sweet perfume drifted down to me. She was the most beautiful thing I'd ever seen in my young life.

My mouth fell open. The others saw me staring and turned to look. Antef gave a soft moan.

There was a rattle of stones as a man in heavy sandals appeared behind the lady. He said, "Don't you peasants kneel when you come before your Queen Ankhesenamen?"

It was Captain Khammale of the palace guard. We fell to our knees in front of Tutankhamen's widow.

"I will have sharp wooden stakes put up by the river," the captain said to the Queen. "I will have the thieves dropped on to the stakes to show all of Thebes what happens to grave robbers." His eyes were bright with the thought of our deaths.

The queen spoke quietly. "No, Khammale. No more deaths. My husband died for the treasures of Egypt. These poor people need not die."

The joy slipped from the face of Captain Khammale. "They must be punished, your Highness."

The sad-faced queen spread her hands. "They hoped to steal a life of laziness," she sighed. "So punish them with a life of work. Set them to work in the fields. I will take the girl to be a handmaiden in my palace."

Dalifa smirked. It was more a reward than a punishment.

"She will scrub and sew until her fingers bleed," Ankhesenamen promised.

Dalifa's smirk slid from her face.

The Captain shook his head. "As you wish, your Highness."

He drew his sword and held it at Antef's throat. "To the river you filthy little thief." He looked at me. "And you too, boy."

He pointed at big Kerpes. "And as for you, you can start filling in that tunnel."

At noon the next day the sun was high and even the crocodiles were too hot to move from the river. But we were working on the shadufs and the fields, pulling at weeds until our backs were breaking and sweat flowed like the Nile.

Just one day before, I had been dreaming of a life of ease and more riches than I could ever spend. One dreadful day later and I had only a nightmare of work and poverty.

The guards let us stop to drink a little weak beer and chew on an onion each. "We were wrong to try and rob the dead, Antef," I moaned as I sank to the ground beside him.

He looked at me quickly. "No. We were not wrong. The only thing we did wrong was getting caught. There was nothing *wrong* with trying to make ourselves rich."

I looked across the fields to the royal palace. "Even the Queen didn't look happy with all her riches," I said.

Antef snorted. "No. They say the new king is Ay, Tutankhamen's uncle. To make the throne his own he will marry little widow-Queen Ankhesenamen."

"He's an old man," I said. "Poor lady."

Antef looked up and slapped my aching shoulders with his horny hand. "He is old! Hah! There's a thought, Paneb!"

"So?"

"So … he will die soon. And when he does, they will bury him with all his wealth. And next time we'll be more careful. We'll make sure we aren't caught!"

A guard cracked a whip and ordered us back to the baked fields.

"Next time?"

Antef grinned his broken-toothed grin. "Next time," he chuckled. "Next time."

Afterword

By 1900 all the kings' tombs of ancient Egypt had been robbed. Some had been robbed soon after the king was buried, some were robbed in modern times.

Then, in 1922, the archaeologist Howard Carter came across a forgotten tomb – the tomb of a young king called Tutankhamen. It was full of the dead King's treasure. But there was a mystery. A tunnel had been dug from the door of the tomb to the outside. In the tunnel was a bag of rings. Someone had broken in to the tomb soon after the king was buried over 3,200 years before.

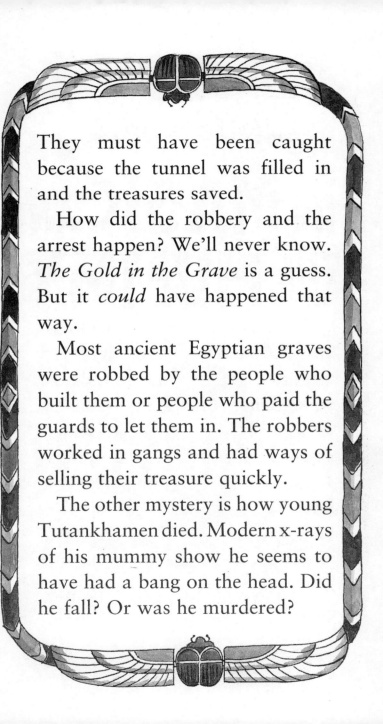

They must have been caught because the tunnel was filled in and the treasures saved.

How did the robbery and the arrest happen? We'll never know. *The Gold in the Grave* is a guess. But it *could* have happened that way.

Most ancient Egyptian graves were robbed by the people who built them or people who paid the guards to let them in. The robbers worked in gangs and had ways of selling their treasure quickly.

The other mystery is how young Tutankhamen died. Modern x-rays of his mummy show he seems to have had a bang on the head. Did he fall? Or was he murdered?

TERRY DEARY'S
EGYPTIAN TALES

THE MAGIC AND THE MUMMY

Illustrated by Helen Flook

A & C BLACK
AN IMPRINT OF BLOOMSBURY
LONDON   NEW DELHI   NEW YORK   SYDNEY

Chapter 1

The House of Death

Neria couldn't sleep.

She lay on the cool floor of her room and wriggled with excitement.

"The House of Death!" she whispered in the dark. "The House of Death!" And she remembered over and over again what her father had told her the night before.

"Neria," he said. "You are a clever girl."

"Thank you father," she muttered and blushed. He hardly ever seemed to notice her. He was a grand priest at the royal temple. He certainly hadn't told her she was clever before. How did he know?

He dusted crumbs of bread off his hands and wiped his thin mouth. His scary, dark eyes looked into her. "I can trust you," he went on.

"Oh, yes, father," she said quietly.

"I have a very special task for you," he said. Her brothers and sisters fell silent and looked at her.

She was the oldest and they always knew she was a special girl. She was like a mother to them since their own mother had died a year ago. Their faces were still but their ears were twitching like hippos on the banks of the Nile.

Neria nodded.

"Tomorrow I am taking you to the House of Death with me," the man said. His shaved head glowed in the golden light of the oil lamps and he looked like a god.

"Oooh!" her youngest brother, Karu, cried. "House of Death! Neria is going to die."

The priest turned his head slowly and_ looked at his little son. The boy gave a hiccup of fear. "The House of Death is not the pace you go to die, my son. It is the place you go after you are dead ... at least the place the great people of Egypt go when they are dead."

The little boy's mouth fell open.
"Oooh!"

"The House of Death is where we
preserve the bodies of people ..."

"What's 'preserve'?" Karu whispered.

Father nodded. "If you have a piece of
meat, and you leave it in the sun, what
happens to it?"

"The cat would pinch it!" the little
boy said.

8

"Or the jackals would come in from the desert and gobble it up."

Father closed his eyes for a moment and took a slow breath. "If you put it on the roof, where the cats and the jackals couldn't get it …"

Karu wriggled. "The birds would eat it."

The priest held the table so tightly his knuckles turned white. Neria tried to shake her head – to tell her little brother to close his mouth before their father lost his temper.

At last their father said. "If we put the meat in a cage, and close the door, so the animals and birds could not eat it, what would happen to it?"

Karu smiled. "Then I would open the door of the cage and I would eat it!"

"No you would NOT!" their father shouted. The children jumped as if a Nile crocodile had snapped its jaws suddenly shut. "I will TELL you what would happen to the meat. It would become slimy and very smelly. It would be covered in flies and the flies would lay their eggs. The eggs would hatch out into maggots and the maggots would eat the meat."

"Do they like slimy, smelly meat?" the boy gasped.

"They *love* it," Father said. "Love it." He turned back to Neria. "People like us would be like pieces of meat when we died. We'd rot and smell and be eaten by maggots. That is why we have to turn people into mummies."

"I know, Father," Neria said.

"That's what we do in the House of Death. We make mummies." He lowered his voice. "We are going to get very busy in the House of Death some day soon. I need some extra help. Someone who can learn quickly. Someone I can trust. I have chosen you, Neria."

The girl felt a warm tingle in her cheeks. "Thank you, Father," she said and lowered her dark eyes.

In the quiet of the room little Karu's voice sounded like a reed pipe. "Will I be made into a mummy, Father, or will I be eaten by maggots?"

Father turned on him with an angry glare. "If you do not close your monkey mouth you will be chopped up and fed to the crocodiles."

14

"Ooooh!" Karu cried. He jumped to his feet in fear, took a step backwards and fell over the cat. The cat squawked, the boy squeaked and the children tried to hide their laughter.

"Get to bed NOW!" Father roared. "Or I will feed you to the Pharaoh's own pet crocodile."

Karu fled, his little legs pattering faster than his thumping heart. He clutched his favourite rag ball to his mouth.

Neria was sure Father's tight mouth was trying not to laugh. At last he looked around the table. "In fact you can all go to bed," he said. "Sleep well, Neria, you have a busy day ahead tomorrow."

But Neria didn't sleep well. She hardly slept at all. Her cat crept onto her blanket and purred like a mountain lion.

She stroked it and whispered, "The House of Death! I'm going to the House of Death, Katkins."

The cat purred.

At last the black night turned to the darkest grey and she knew Horus the Hawk God was opening his eye. The eye that was the sun.

It was time to go.

Chapter 2

Fate of the Pharaoh

Neria's father was dressed in his finest robes today. He marched down the middle of the road and everyone scurried to get out of his way. It was as if he was too bright to look at; bright as the eye of Horus. Even the dogs tucked in their tails and ran.

Neria walked a little way behind him. Suddenly a woman ran out from a dark doorway. She threw her arms up to the sky and shrieked. Then she bent down to the ground, grabbed a fistful of dust and let it trickle over her grey-black hair.

Neria's father nodded. "So, it has started. We must hurry." He strode out and the girl trotted to his side.

"What has started, Father?"

"The woman must have heard some news. Last night the Pharaoh was sick. This morning he must be dead." He marched on. "We have work to do."

They headed east towards the rising sun, passed through the poorer streets of shambling houses and then through the city gates. Guards raised their spears to salute them.

Neria copied her father; she raised her chin and ignored them.

This gate led into the desert and ahead of them stood the House of Death. Not a house at all. A fine white tent that had no walls. All the smells could be blown away on the desert breeze. Perfumes of cedar and rose took away the smell of death but still the jackals on the hills caught the scent. They watched and waited.

Inside the House of Death dozens of men and women hurried about their tasks. When Neria's father came near they stopped and bowed.

There were twenty tables under the rippling white roof and every one had a body on it. The priest walked up to a man in a black robe and said, "Has it started, Thekel?"

Thekel was a large man with a small, round head. It was shaved and his ears stuck out like handles on a water jug. He smiled happily.

"It has started, Lord. The old Pharaoh became a god last night at moonrise. They're dumping his body here later on today."

Neria's father pulled a face as if cheerful Thekel's words had hurt. He turned and said, "This is my daughter, Neria. She'll deal with Bastet."

Neria was puzzled. She knew that Bastet was the cat-god who looked after their corn.

Thekel grinned his simple grin. "We need all the hands we can get."

"Teach her what to do," her father ordered.

"Leave it to me. Let's start with the brain-pulling, shall we?" he asked.

Before Neria could answer, her father said, "No! Wait. If the Pharaoh's body is arriving this afternoon we need to get Nesumontu out of the way. Let's do it now."

Thekel winked at Neria. "Won't be long, mistress. I'll have him gutted in no time."

He clapped his hands and the priests gathered round. "Right, my Lords. We need to get Nesumontu ripped open. Let's make it snappy ... as the crocodile said to the fish."

The priests shuffled around one table where the body of a withered old man lay. They began to chant a prayer and their voices filled the tent.

They looked to the east where light from the eye of Horus was pouring in to the tent.

Neria shuddered when she saw the great god Anubis walk out of the sun and towards the body. He had the body of a man but the big-eared, sharp-nosed head of a monstrous jackal.

Neria had expected to see the dead here. But this was a shock. This was Anubis ... the God of the Dead himself.

Chapter 3
The First Mummy

Anubis walked between the tables and stumbled. He caught his toe on the leg of a table. The leg cracked, the table fell and the mummy of a man rolled onto the floor.

"Ohhhh!" Anubis roared with pain and anger. He raised his hands, grasped his ears and pulled. Neria blinked as Anubis pulled his head off.

But the head of Anubis was just a mask. Under the mask was the red and angry face of her father. "I hate this mask," he grumbled as the chanting of the priests became a jumble of noise and stuttered to an end. "Can't see a blind thing."

He threw the mask to the ground and limped to the table where the old man's body lay. "Has someone scooped out the brain?"

A young priest held up a bowl of grey mush. "Yes, Lord."

"We're in a hurry," Neria's father said. He looked at the body. "Sorry, Nesumontu," he sighed. "I'll have to do you without the mask."

A priest handed Neria's father a pen made from a reed and a pot of ink. He marked a line about the length of his hand on the old man's side then turned to the man in black. "Right, Thekel, get on with it!"

Thekel took a sharp stone knife from his belt and sliced along the line her father had just drawn. He plunged his hand into the body, wriggled it around and quickly pulled out the stomach. A priest took it and wrapped it in a cloth. He took it off to a stone jar and plopped it in.

They did the same with the liver, kidneys, lungs and guts. When Thekel was finished, the priests began to jeer at him.

Thekel grinned and said, "Thanks, lads. But can we cut it short? We're in a hurry today."

"Oh, all right," they agreed and went back to their jobs.

Thekel turned to Neria. "Right mistress, I need to give you a quick lesson in making a mummy."

"But why did they call you all those names?" she asked. "Didn't you mind?"

"Nah!" he chuckled. "It's an unclean job. I do it and they have to drive me out of the House of Death because I am an unclean man. Just a sort of game really. Now I'll just wash the blood off my hands and I'll show you round."

By the end of the morning Neria knew most of the things that went on in the House of Death. The bodies that had been emptied, like old Nesumontu's, were washed with palm wine – inside and out – then they were ready to be dried out.

"We cover the body in this salty stuff – natron," Thekel explained. "We leave it for forty days until it's dry as a desert beetle's back, then we wrap it in bandages to make a mummy."

Neria nodded towards a boy who was writing on parchment pieces. "What's he doing?"

"Writing the Book of the Dead – prayers that are wrapped in the bandages. They help the dead person in the next life. The gods must be clever enough to read them. I never learned to read or write."

"Neither did I," Neria said.

"Never mind." Thekel shrugged. "You won't have to. Here is your table. All you have to do is turn Bastet into a mummy."

Neria was just about to ask, "Who's Bastet?" when she heard a loud noise and it was getting louder. "What's that sound?"

"Trumpets," Thekel said. "The Pharaoh is coming. Here we go! Stand by your tables, lads!"

Chapter 4
Cruel for Cats

Soldiers marched into the tent carrying the Pharaoh in a cloth cradle slung between two poles.

Neria's father met the men and led them to an empty table. The girl saw that a cat was marching with the soldiers, tail held high and proud as if it was the Pharaoh himself.

Suddenly Thekel swooped and picked up the startled cat. He carried it carefully over to Neria's table. "Here you are, Mistress. This is Bastet. It is your job to turn him into a mummy."

"The cat? The Pharaoh named his cat after the god? And you want me to turn it into a mummy?"

"Of course. The Pharaoh had his holy cat when he was alive. He has to have it with him in his tomb. They will go to the Afterlife together."

Neria blinked. "I know animal mummies go in tombs with their masters – but this one is still alive. I can't turn a live cat into a mummy."

Thekel grinned his wide and happy grin. "I know."

"So, what do I do?" Neria frowned.

"Kill it!"

The cat was the colour of warm sand and its eyes were as pure as gold. It stood on her table and looked up at her. It stretched its neck and rubbed its head against her chin. It looked just like Katkins.

"Here's my knife," Thekel said.

Neria took the cold, black blade. The cat purred. Tears began to prickle her eyes. "I – I can't!"

Thekel shrugged. "You have to. Your father will be very upset if the Pharaoh's cat doesn't go into the tomb with him."

"I can't," Neria said stupidly. "What am I going to do?"

The big man with the small head looked at her tenderly. "You know the story of Osiris? The first mummy?"

Neria nodded. "Osiris was killed by his brother and chopped into 13 pieces. His wife gathered all the pieces together and used magic to bring him back to life for a little while. And then she wrapped the 13 pieces as a mummy so his spirit could go to the Afterlife."

Thekel shook his head. "Not exactly. His wife only found 12 pieces. A crocodile had eaten one! So she replaced the lost bit with a piece of wood." He lowered his voice. "We do it in here – if an arm falls off we replace it with a piece of wood. We wrap it in bandages and no one ever notices."

The cat purred and looked up at the man. Neria stroked it and frowned. "So?"

"What if we lost a whole body – or a whole cat?" he whispered.

"You'd … you'd have to wrap up a whole mummy full of wood," she breathed.

Thekel spread his hands wide, grinned and said nothing. He looked at the cat. The cat looked back.

Neria snatched the cat from the table, tucked it under her arm and ran from the tent. Everyone was fussing about the Pharaoh. No one but Thekel saw her go.

She raced across the desert, through the city gate, down the crowded street and into her house.

Neria dropped the grumbling cat into a wooden chest in her room. A moment later she was back to drop in a piece of dried fish then closed the lid.

She raced around the house and gathered up anything useful she could find – wooden spoons and even Karu's wooden crocodile on wheels. She still needed something round, and about the size of her fist, to make the head.

Karu was playing in the garden alone. He was throwing his rag ball up in the air and catching it. "Karu!" Neria cried. "Throw me your ball."

The little boy shook his head. "No. It's my ball."

"I'll show you a wonderful game."

"No," he said and stuck out his bottom lip.

Neria knew she didn't have much time. "I'll ... I'll use magic and turn it into something wonderful!"

Karu narrowed his eyes. "What?"

"A cat! A cat like my Katkins. You've always wanted one."

"You can't do magic," the little boy sniffed.

"Urrrrgh!" Neria cried angrily. She marched up to Karu, snatched the ball from his podgy little hand and ran.

She was racing down the road and could hear his wailing until she was half way to the city gates.

Chapter 5

The Magic Cat

As the Eye of Horus sank in the sky the desert grew dark with purple shadows. Neria trotted back home behind her father. "You did well," he said.

"Thank you father," she said.

"The mummy you made from the cat Bastet was fine – for a first try."

"Thank you father."

"Very neat."

They walked through the city gates.
The guards saluted and closed the gates
to shut out the jackals of the night.
When they reached their house, Karu was
waiting for them. His scowling face was
streaked with mud and tears.

Father ignored him. The boy cried out, "Father, Father! Neria stole my ball – she took it and she ..." Karu stopped shouting. It's hard to shout when your big sister has a hand across your mouth.

She dragged the boy down the hall and into her room. Karu struggled all the way. There was just enough light in her room to see the chest in the corner. She took her hand away from her brother's mouth.

"Where's my ball?" he sobbed.

"I haven't got it."

"Waaaagh! Why not?"

"I told you," she hissed. "I used magic to turn it into a cat."

Karu stopped crying suddenly. "No you didn't."

"Yes I did."

"Where is it?" he demanded.

"In that chest," she said.

He ran over to the corner of the room and heaved up the lid. A dazed cat blinked up at him. "Ohhhh!" Karu breathed. "A cat."

"Your cat," Neria told him.

Karu lifted the cat out carefully and clutched it in his short arms. "A magic cat," he said.

Neria smiled. "A magic cat. Now let's wash your face and go to dinner."

As the servants lit the lamps in the dining room Karu walked in with a scrubbed and happy face. "Neria," he said.

"Yes, Karu?"

"I think you stole my crocodile on wheels."

"So?"

"So I would like you to magic me a bow and arrow, a fishing boat and a golden bowl for my cat."

Neria smiled sweetly at her brother. "Karu. You have your cat. Ask me for anything else and I will turn you into a mummy."

"You can't do that!" he squawked.

"Oh, yes I can – Father says I make a fine mummy, a neat mummy."

Her teeth and eyes glinted in the lamplight. Karu looked up at her and was afraid. He swallowed hard, turned pale and began to shake.

"It's alright, Neria. You can keep my crocodile," he said.

"I think that's best," she said softly. "Mummy knows best."

Afterword

The House of Death wasn't a house at all. It was a large tent where the mummy was made ready for its last journey – the journey into the Afterlife.

The Afterlife was a lovely place to live if you were lucky enough, and good enough, to get there. It was away from the heat of the desert and the smell of death – away from the jackals that wanted to steal the king's flesh and the humans who wanted to steal his riches.

The House of Death was a holy place and a work place. The priest in charge was a servant of the jackal god, Anubis. So, of course, this one priest wore the Jackal mask over his head. Anubis was the good god who looked over mummies and guarded their tombs. His priest led the chanting of all the priests and that was the sign for the start of the mummy-making.

The king could not go along to the Afterlife without his loyal pets. They had to be killed and turned into mummies too so they could be buried with him.

The priest of Anubis would be one of the most important men in the city, his house would be fine and his family would be rich.

THE
PHANTOM AND
THE FISHERMAN

Illustrated by Helen Flook

A & C BLACK
AN IMPRINT OF BLOOMSBURY
LONDON NEW DELHI NEW YORK SYDNEY

Chapter 1

The Miserable Master

"Do you believe in ghosts?"
Menes whispered to his
friend Ahmose.

Menes heard the sudden swish of a stick then felt it strike him on the back.

"No talking in class!" the fat and sweating teacher hissed.

"Sorry, Master Meshwesh," Menes muttered. He bent his head over the plaster board in front of him. He dipped his reed pen in water, rubbed it against the black ink-block and started writing again.

Lessons were in a cool garden with a sparkling fountain. But still Menes sweated over his work.

5

But fat Master Meshwesh wasn't
finished with him yet.

"You will never be a good scribe if you
talk when you should be working, will
you, Menes?"

"No, Master Meshwesh," the boy
sighed.

"But, if you work hard, you will grow
to be a temple scribe and as rich as a lord.
You'd like that, wouldn't you, Menes?"

"Yes, Master Meshwesh."

The teacher was panting in the midday sun and licking his thick lips.

"Yes, Master Meshwesh," he mimicked.

"Rich. Learn to write and you can become a priest. Or even a corn dealer, like Ahmose's father. Not like your father. A poor and stinking fisherman. If you talk in class I'll have you thrown out of school and you'll end up like your fishy, foul father."

Suddenly the master grabbed Menes by the ear and lifted the boy to his feet. He breathed his onion breath into the boy's face. "Have you brought any fish from home for me?"

"Yes, Master Meshwesh!" Menes squealed as the fat thumb and finger squeezed his ear.

"Good," the teacher said. "In that case we will stop for lunch."

The ten boys rinsed their pens in the water, stood up and stretched. Menes opened his linen bag and took out two pieces of dried fish and some bread. The teacher let loose the boy's ear, snatched the food in one huge paw and grinned his gap-toothed grin.

"Tasty!" he said and smacked his lips.

"One fish was for me," Menes said.

"Well, I've just taken it from you as a punishment," Master Meshwesh said. He walked over to the shade of a garden wall and began to fill his face with the food in one hand then wash it down with a flask of beer in the other.

The boys knew he would sleep for an hour after lunch as he did every day. They would be free to talk.

Menes shook his head. "Tell me, Ahmose, do you think learning to write will make us rich?"

Ahmose was the same age as Menes but his father was a wealthy corn dealer. "If we can write, the temple will pay us well to work. Maybe one of the lords will give us a job. Yes, being a scribe will make us rich."

"So why is Master Meshwesh a teacher? Why isn't he making money at the temple?" Menes asked.

Ahmose took his friend by the arm and dragged him round the corner of the garden wall so they were hidden from the bullying master.

He spoke quickly and quietly. "He was the scribe to Payneshi, the governor of our region. He had to keep a record of all the corn and the animals, the gold and the jewels, the slaves and the wine of Payneshi."

"An important job," Menes said.

"But Master Meshwesh used his scribe skills to cheat Payneshi. If Payneshi got two bags of gold then Meshwesh wrote that he had *one* bag of gold, you see?"

Menes shook his head. "No."

"Meshwesh wrote one bag of gold on the list – and there was one bag of gold in Payneshi's counting house. The other bag of gold would go into Meshwesh's pocket, you see?"

"Did he have big pockets?" Menes
asked.

Ahmose groaned. "I don't mean he put
it in his pocket – I mean he pinched it.
He was caught when the Pharaoh sent a
box of jewels to Payneshi and then sent a
message to ask if Payneshi liked them."

"Did he?" Menes asked.

"He never got them! Payneshi realised Meshwesh must have stolen them," Ahmose explained. "He was furious."

"Did he get the box of jewels back?" Menes asked.

"No. Meshwesh must have hidden them. He said he knew nothing about them. Payneshi banished Meshwesh from the city of Karnak for five years. Now he's back to torment us. No one trusts him – no one will give him a scribe job – so he has to be a teacher," Ahmose said. "See?"

Menes shook his head. "No."

"No?"

"If he really did hide the treasure then he'd just go and find it."

"Maybe he forgot where it was," Ahmose said.

"Would you forget where you'd hidden a fortune?" Menes asked.

Ahmose shook his head. "It's a mystery … and talking about mysteries why did you ask if I believed in ghosts?"

"Because there's a foul phantom in the new house at the temple gate," Menes said. "Old Maiarch is being driven from her home. I have to use my scribe skills. And I have to kill it!"

Chapter 2

The Fearful Phantom

Ahmose shuddered even though the noon-day sun was scorching the street. "How do you know the phantom won't kill *you*?" he asked.

Menes shrugged. "It's a chance I have to take." He peered round the corner of the wall. Master Meshwesh was dozing in the shade. "Come with me."

"Are we going to see the ghost?"

"We are going to see old Maiarch," Menes said as he led the way down the cool alleys that led to the Temple of Horus.

"Is she dead?"

"No, but she nearly died of fright when she saw the phantom," Menes said. "She woke up in the middle of a moonless night and saw him. Just a shape in the starlight. He was big as an ox. He roared like a hippo when she woke up."

"You can't kill a phantom – not a monster like that," Ahmose said. "You're a scribe, not a soldier."

Menes laughed. "And it's my reed pen I'm going to use to kill him," he said.

"You can't stab a phantom with a reed pen," Ahmose argued.

Menes hurried on. "When the king dies they wrap him as a mummy. And inside the wrapping they put the Book of the Dead."

"The book is full of prayers that will help the spirit in the afterlife. Protect it from the monsters that are waiting there to attack it. We all need a Book of the Dead – even if we aren't rich enough to be made into mummies."

Ahmose nodded. "I've heard about the monsters. There's a snake that spits poison at you."

"And boiling hot lakes," Menes reminded him.

"Rivers of fire."

"And at the end of it all there's the Devourer waiting for you. Part crocodile, part hippo and part lion. If you've been evil he rips out your heart and eats it!" Menes cried.

"That's why people need us so much. We can write the prayers that will help them."

Ahmose smiled. "I see. You have written prayers for Maiarch to drive away the phantom."

"I have," Menes said. "She promised to pay me well. Maybe enough to buy my dad a new boat. Without a boat he can't fish. Without fish to sell my family will starve."

"I could lend you money," Ahmose said.

Menes gripped his arm. "Thanks, friend. But it would be better if I could earn it myself. Maybe she'll pay me today."

They turned a corner into the great paved square in front of the temple.

"This is Maiarch's house," Menes said, leading the way through an arch into a fine garden. There was a large pond with golden fish swimming in sparkling water. Trees gave shade and flowers covered the grass. "Maiarch is very rich," Menes explained. "She had this new house built just for herself."

"It's even bigger than our house," Ahmose said.

The boys walked into the shadowy darkness of the house. An ancient woman lay on a low couch. Her skin was wrinkled and pale as old parchment. Her eyes were bright as a bird's.

"Good day, Maiarch," Menes said. "This is my friend Ahmose."

"Sit down, sit down," the old woman croaked. The boys sat on the floor.

"Did it work?" Menes asked.

"Did it work? he says. Did it work? It did not. Hopeless. Useless. Worthless scrap of parchment."

"The phantom came back?"

"The phantom came back? he says. Came back? He came back twice as large, twice as ugly and twice as evil. He says that if I'm still here when he comes back tonight he'll crush me like a scarab beetle. And he could too. He's big enough to crush a crocodile."

The old woman spread her arms wide to show how big the phantom was. Suddenly she swept her arms forward and pointed at Menes. "So you needn't think I am paying you anything, young scribe. You're hopeless, useless, worthless."

Chapter 3

The Greedy Ghost

Menes sniffed away a tear. "I'll try again," he offered.

"He'll try again!" Maiarch cackled. "Well you won't try your silly prayers. They're hopeless, useless, worthless."

"Maybe we could try something else," Ahmose put in.

"Someone will have to do something," the old woman moaned. "The gods will be very angry."

"Uh? Why?" Ahmose asked.

"Why? he says. Why? Because the phantom didn't just disturb my sleep and threaten me. He walked up to my altar ... see it there?"

The boys looked at the wall behind them. A lamp lit the stone statue of the god Bes – an ugly dwarf.

"Bes looks after women and children," Menes said.

"He's supposed to – my old legs won't get me to the temple, so I have my own altar in the house. Every day I put fish, bread and beer on the altar for Bes."

"Does he eat it?" Menes asked. He'd always wanted to know what happened to the food offered to the gods in the temple. They seemed to eat a lot.

"He doesn't usually eat it," Maiarch said. "But last night he didn't even have the chance. When the phantom had finished frightening me he walked up to the altar and pinched all the fish and bread and beer. The cheek of it. He packed it in his mouth and said he'd be back tonight."

"That's no phantom," Ahmose said. "Phantoms don't eat fish. They eat human spirits. I don't think you have a ghost, old lady."

"Here! Here! Here! Watch who you're calling old," Maiarch squawked. "I'm only sixty summers old – King Pepi lived to a hundred or more."

Ahmose sighed. "What I'm saying is you have a common thief. He's just trying to scare you so he can rob you."

Menes shook his head. "But why doesn't he just take what he wants. Old Maiarch can't stop him."

"Now *you're* calling me 'old', you young monkey," Maiarch moaned.

Ahmose nodded slowly. "So, what does he want?"

"The best way to find out is to ask him," Menes said.

Ahmose's mouth fell open. "You think a thief will stop and chat?"

"He will if we've captured him. If we make him talk," Menes said. "We'll be here tonight. We'll grab him and force him to talk."

"He's stronger than an ox," Ahmose reminded him.

"Big enough to crush a crocodile," Maiarch added.

"Don't worry," Menes told them. "I have a fool-proof plan."

"Better than your hopeless, useless, worthless scrap of parchment?" the old woman asked.

"Much better."

"What's the plan?" Ahmose asked.

"I'll tell you after school," Menes promised.

Chapter 4

Opet and Beer

At the end of the afternoon Menes raced through the city, over the fields and down to the small house of baked mud at the edge of the Nile.

His father was trying to patch his old boat with reeds while his younger sisters worked on mending the nets.

His mother was pouring beer from a large stone jar – straining it through a linen cloth into a bowl. "What's wrong with your back?" she asked when she saw her son's red and purple marks.

He shrugged. "Master Meshwesh beat me for talking."

"I know teachers are told to beat bad boys," she sighed, "but Meshwesh seems to enjoy it. Let me get you some beer and bread for dinner."

"I'll have this," Menes said, reaching for the bowl.

"No you won't!" his father cried. "That is extra strong beer. It's for the Festival of Opet tonight. I've been waiting for weeks to taste that beer. That would knock out an ox, that beer!"

"Would it?" Menes murmured. He took the jug of weak beer and swallowed hungrily.

His mother smiled. "You are a growing boy. You enjoy your food. I wish we had more."

He would have had more if Meshwesh hadn't stolen his lunch.

"Sorry, no fresh fish today," his father said. "I'd be crocodile-food if I tried to go out in this," he added and gave the old boat a kick.

"Never mind," Menes' mother told his father. "Tonight you can join the Festival of Opet. Forget your cares for a while. Are you coming to the temple with us, Menes?"

The boy licked the last crumb from his fingers and said, "No. I am going to make us rich tonight. I'm going to buy Father a new boat."

His mother laughed. "You're a good boy. That would be nice." But he could tell she didn't believe him.

As darkness fell his father and mother went into the house to put on their ragged clothes, but the best they had. Menes poured the strong beer into a flask and replaced it with weak beer. "Sorry, Father," he whispered.

His parents left as the star Sirius rose in the sky. "The goddess Isis is looking down on us. Time to go," his father said.

When he was sure his sisters were playing happily in the house, Menes gathered up his father's net and his writing tools and followed his parents down the dark road to the city. It was time to meet and defeat the phantom.

Chapter 5

The Fallen Phantom

The square in front of the temple was crowded with people. The noise would wake a mummy in its tomb. The priests of the temple of Karnak carried a statue of the god Amun into the square where it met another group of priests carrying the statue of the goddess Mut.

The people cheered when the two
statues met and the drinking began.
Menes pushed his way through to the
gateway of Maiarch's house. In the
shadows he saw Ahmose waiting for him.

"Is Maiarch safely out of the way?"
Menes asked.

"My father has offered her a bed at
our house for the Opet Festival," he
said. "She grumbled, but she went. Our
servants carried her."

"On with the plan, then," Menes said. "Get on to the couch, wear the old woman's wig and I'll hide in that chest."

The boys hurried to set up their trap and then they waited.

The only light was the lamp by the statue of the god Bes. His ugly face glowed and watched as Menes placed the large bowl of strong beer in front of him. "Sorry, Bes, but it's not for you!"

Ahmose lay on the couch while Menes climbed into the chest and held his reed pen and a piece of parchment. "I'll make a note of everything he says. Then we'll go to the governor and have him arrested."

The noise of the crowd outside roared and swirled around them. So they didn't hear the phantom when he arrived. "Still here, old woman?" the voice roared.

Ahmose jumped.

Menes peered out from the lid of the chest and made out the figure of a large man with a black cloth over his head to hide his face. There were holes cut out for his mouth and eyes.

Ahmose called back, "Here! Here! Here! Watch who you're calling 'old'. I'm only sixty summers old – King Pepi lived to a hundred or more."

"You're old enough to be my granny," the phantom snarled.

"No I'm not, you young monkey!" Ahmose said and his voice was perfect.

"Look, you withered old baboon, if I can't scare you out then I'll have to throw you out," he said and moved towards the couch.

"Phantoms can't hurt the living," Ahmose told him.

"No?"

"No! You're just a spirit. You can't pick me up."

"Yes I can! I'm an extra-strong spirit."

"Prove it."

"How?"

"Let me see ... pick up that bowl of beer by the statue of Bes," Ahmose said and waved a shaking finger towards the statue by the lamp.

The phantom wandered across to the table and picked up the bowl of strong beer. "See? Told you!" he crowed.

"But I'll bet you can't drink it," Ahmose urged.

"Watch me," the phantom said and sipped the beer.

"Ooooh! Nice drop of beer that," he said smacking his lips. "I've had a few tonight but none as nice and strong as this." He put it to his lips and swallowed it all.

Then he stepped back. He seemed to catch his heel on the rush mat and sat down heavily. "Oooof!" he grunted then belched. He swayed. "Ooooh! Just have a little sit down, I think."

The big body swayed and the mask hung crookedly so he was looking out through one eye and the mouth-hole.

"Just sit down? You didn't come here to sit down. You came to rob me, you villain!" Ahmose cried.

"Rob 'oo," the phantom said. "Not rob 'oo. Just come to get what belongs to me."

Menes slowly raised the lid of the chest further. He put down the pen and picked up the net.

The phantom didn't seem to notice. He was too busy trying to talk to Ahmose on the old woman's couch. And talking was hard because the words were getting muddled in his mouth.

"What belongs to you, you villain?"
Ahmose asked as Menes crept around
behind him.

"Me tresher ... me trea-sure. I buried
it here five summers ago before I was
banished from Karnak. I hid it under the
floor of me house. But when I came back I
found you'd knocked down me house and
built yours in its place."

Suddenly the large man began to sob. "Me tresher! Me lovely tresher. All I want's me treeeesher! Waaaagggghhhh!"

And to soak up the tears he pulled off the mask.

Ahmose jumped from the bed as Menes jumped from the shadows to throw the net over the fat man. "Master Meshwesh!" the boys cried.

"Wesh mesh?" the man bubbled. "Wish-wash, mess-mish!"

As Menes tied the rope tightly the fat teacher rolled on to the floor and began to snore.

Chapter 6
The Terrible Teacher

The governor's guards came and took the terrible teacher away. That night they dug up the treasure and returned it to their master, Payneshi.

The next day Meshwesh was dragged in front of the governor. "I should have you beaten to death, Meshwesh," he said.

"Yes, governor," Meshwesh groaned.

"And I should give the beating job to the young scribes." The whole school was there to see the trial. "Would you like that boys?" Payneshi asked.

"Yes!" the boys roared.

"But really it is for Menes and Ahmose to decide. You are theirs to deal with as they please. If they want you chopped into fifty pieces and thrown to the crocodiles then that is what I will order."

The fat teacher looked at the boys, his red eyes puffed and pitiful. "It would hurt."

Menes looked at Ahmose then up at Payneshi the judge. "Spare him," Menes said quietly. "He's really taught us a lot – he's a very good scribe but not a very good man – and he's been punished. He's lost his treasure."

Payneshi blinked. "It's *my* treasure."

"Sorry," Menes said quickly. "Spare him. Let him go back to teaching us … but take his beating sticks away."

Payneshi said, "A wise young man and a generous one."

"Very generous," Meshwesh whined.

"But I can be generous too," Payneshi said. "I am giving you half of all the treasure that Meshwesh stole. It is your reward."

And so Menes walked from the palace a rich young man.

"What will you buy?" his mother asked him when he reached home.

"A boat for Dad," he said.

"I should think so too," his father grumbled. "You owe it to me."

Mother threw her head back and laughed. "You stole his strong beer. He loves strong spirits. We got to the festival and he took a drink. All he tasted was weak beer. He nearly choked."

"Ah," Menes said wisely. "Just like the phantom who drank it – he thought he was a strong spirit too!"

Afterword

Scribes had to be experts at Egyptian picture-writing – hieroglyphics. We have to learn twenty-six letters in our alphabet. Scribes had to learn seven hundred signs.

So, school was hard and the teachers were strict. It seems schoolboys could be lazy and easily bored ... just like today really. Teachers were told to beat boys because beating was the best way to make them work.

Once a boy had learned how to be a scribe he could have the best jobs in Egypt – in the king's palace or in the temples. While peasants sweated in the fields the scribes had a comfortable and rich life. School was tough and sometimes painful – but it was worth it in the end.

The Egyptians believed in the spirit world. Evil forces were all around them. The best way to protect yourself from an evil spirit (or a ghost) was with a prayer. If that prayer was written down by a scribe then it was even more powerful. Of course a scribe would charge you for writing the spell.

Thieves like Meshwesh were often banished from their homes and sent away to try and survive in another town where they had no friends to help them.

THE PLOT ON THE PYRAMID

Illustrated by Helen Flook

A & C BLACK
AN IMPRINT OF BLOOMSBURY
LONDON NEW DELHI NEW YORK SYDNEY

Chapter 1

River and Rat

Nephoris sat by the edge of the mud-brown river and threw a stone into it. She was a tall girl and made her little brother Pere look tiny.

A light wind kept her cool and the rustling reeds seemed the only sound in the world. "Perfect," she said.

Of course that was before her mother called her home.

"River," Pere said. He picked up a stone and tried to copy Nephoris's throwing. But he forgot to let go and threw himself into the dirty water.

Nephoris shook her head, paddled into the cool water and pulled him out.

"It's Akhet," she told him.

The little boy's round face crinkled into a frown. "No Akhet. River."

She sat beside him and watched the graceful ibis birds land and stalk through the shallows, looking for food.

"I mean it's the time of the year – Akhet. The time when the river rises. It floods our fields and makes the corn grow. Akhet brings us food."

"Food," Pere repeated. Pere liked food.

Nephoris smiled. There weren't many restful days like this. Days when she could sit in the sun and play with Pere.

She had
to weed
the fields ...

... fetch water ...

... grind corn or
bake bread.

She'd done it ever since she was as young as Pere. But not at Akhet.

"When Akhet comes we can't work in the fields. So we get days like today. Peaceful days," she sighed.

Of course that was before her mother called her home. In the years to come Nephoris would never think of Akhet as the peaceful time again.

Pere took a fistful of mud and made it into a little pile. "Pyramid," he said.

Nephoris nodded. "Yes, Daddy is working on the pyramid for the King. Most of the men of Lisht are helping to build it because they can't work in the fields at Akhet. Poor Dad. We have idle days and he works harder than ever."

Pere made his chubby hand into a fist and smashed it down on top of his mud pile. "Pyramid!" he giggled.

"Poor pyramid," Nephoris said. "King Amenemhat is our god, you know. He makes the river flood the fields and makes the corn grow. That's why we are building Amenemhat a huge pyramid. Build Amenemhat another pyramid," she said.

As Pere piled up the mud, a ripple from the river washed it away. The river was rising fast now. Amenemhat was doing his magic.

Pere frowned at the river and his ruined pyramid. "Naughty!" he said and slapped the water. It splashed up and soaked his angry face. Nephoris laughed. Life was good.

Then her mother called her home.

Her shrill voice carried over the quiet fields. "Da-fi-aaaa!"

10

"Mama!" Pere said and struggled to his feet. He had sharp ears and heard her first. Nephoris quickly washed his muddy legs and hands, scooped him up and ran along the dusty path towards their small mud house.

Meanwhile...

At the Pyramid of Lisht their father, Yenini was getting more and more angry ...

Chapter 2

Peril at the Pyramid

Yenini's face was red. Red with the heat of the midday sun. Red with the strain of pulling a pyramid block almost to the top of Amenemhat's pyramid. But, most of all, red with rage. Rage at the fat little bully, Antef.

Thirty men from Lisht made up a team of workers – the Boat Gang, they called themselves. They were proud of being the best of the hundred gangs that worked on the pyramid.

But the Pharaoh had put Antef in charge – Antef with his perfumed wig and beard-wig, pot belly and wicked tongue.

The Boat Gang were free men. They worked for the love of King Amenemhat. Antef treated them like slaves – like the prisoners of war who were forced to work and beaten.

The day had started badly. Their massive stone, big as a house, had slipped off the barge that carried it over the Nile. They had to fasten ropes around it and drag it through the mud and onto the shore.

Yenini was a little worried that they would not get it up the pyramid before sunset. He didn't like the Boat Gang to fail. They never had before.

Then they heaved it onto a wooden sledge and the sledge cracked. It was an old one and Antef should have got them a better one.

Yenini was a bit upset by that.

The cracked sledge was harder to pull and it took them most of the morning to get it to the foot of the pyramid. Yenini was getting hungry. He had a lunch bag at his belt. When the sun passed the peak of the pyramid they could take a rest and eat in the shadowed side of the tomb.

But the sledge stuck on the ramp that led to the top.

Yenini was annoyed.

"Come on, Boat Gang," he cried. "Put your backs into it. There's a neat little hole at the top just waiting for this stone. And there's an even bigger hole in my stomach waiting for my dinner!"

The men laughed and tried harder. They sweated and strained and the huge stone moved upwards.

That was when Antef really upset them.
He walked behind them and watched
them.

"Laughing are you? Laughing. You are
the biggest bunch of brainless beetles on
this pyramid and all you can do is laugh.
You can't move one little stone and you
think it's funny?" he jeered and cracked
his leather whip. It snapped in the air
close to Yenini's nose.

"Hang on, Antef," Yenini said. "It's your fault that we have this cracked old sledge. It's your job to see we get the best." He was getting angry.

The stone reached the edge of the hole and the Boat Gang began to turn it so it would slide down neatly into the space.

Antef shook his whip in Yenini's face. "I am the servant of Amenemhat. It is the King who tells me what my job is. It's not your job to tell me my job. It's my job to tell you your job," he gabbled. "That's my job and I'm doing my job – so you do your job or my job will be to send you to the King to be punished."

"Don't threaten me," Yenini roared.
He let go of the rope and stepped towards
Antef. The little man jumped back in fear.
His foot slipped on the edge of the hole
and he slipped back into it.

The hole was just too deep for him
to climb out. "Throw me a rope you
desert snakes, you river rats, you savage
scorpions you ... you ... slimy ox dung!"

Yenini was red with rage. "It is time for lunch."

"You take lunch when I say you can take lunch! The King is coming this afternoon. He wants to see this stone in place. You will *not* stop for lunch. I forbid it," Antef wailed. "Get me out of here!"

The Boat Gang looked at each other. They dropped the ropes and walked back down the pyramid for a rest.

Meanwhile...

Back in the village Nephoris was carrying Pere home ...

Chapter 3

The Slipping Stone

Yenini's family lived in a village on the edge of Lisht. That morning the people were working in the shade of the houses but one man worked in the full glare of the sun.

Using precious cedar wood, the artist Oneney was building a large statue.

"Big man," Pere said.

"Statue," Nephoris explained. "It's a statue of King Amenemhat. When he dies the statue will go inside the pyramid with the King's mummy."

The King's statue was almost finished. It was dressed in a white kilt and carrying a shepherd's crook. The life-sized model had one leg raised as if it was striding forward.

Beside it stood a finished model. A small round man in a wig, beard wig and purple robes, no taller than Nephoris.

"That's a model of Antef, the work-driver" Nephoris told her brother. "That will go in the pyramid too, so the dead King has company. Dad doesn't like Antef."

"Naughty man," Pere said and slapped the model.

Oneney was painting the crown on Amenemhat's head a bright red. A bowl was full of red paint.

"Blood," Pere said as Nephoris carried him past the artist.

Oneney shook his head. "No, young Pere. Beetles. I crush beetles to make the red colour."

Nephoris shuddered but Pere just looked puzzled.

"Your mother is looking for you," Oneney told her.

"I heard her calling. What does she want?" Nephoris asked.

Oneney shrugged.

Nephoris's mother stood at the door of their house holding a small package wrapped in cloth.

"What's wrong?" Nephoris asked.

Her mother held out the parcel. "Last night the cat caught a rat and left it in the middle of the floor – a nice present for us. I didn't want Pere picking it up and chewing at it. You know what he's like …"

"Rat," Pere said and licked his lips.

"This morning your father set off for the pyramid to work and I packed him some bread and onion like I always do," her mother went on.

"Yes," Nephoris said.

"Well ... when I went to throw the rat away I opened the parcel and found the bread and onion!" she moaned.

"So," Nephoris grinned, "when Dad opens his lunch parcel he'll find ..."

"Rat!" Pere said.

"Exactly! He'll be furious! He's in a bad temper all the time these days. That Antef bullies the workers all day long from sunrise to sunset. Your dad comes home and he's full of fury. If he goes without food all day he will be as horrible as ... as ... "

"Rat," Pere said.

"Exactly," Mother agreed. "A big, bad-tempered rat." She looked up at the clear sky. The sun was not far from its highest point. "They'll be stopping soon for a break," she said. "You have to get this food to him before they stop!"

"Don't worry, Mum," Nephoris said. "I can run faster than anyone in this village. Give me the food."

She put her brother on the ground, took the parcel and sped towards the site of the pyramid.

The sun ran on. Nephoris ran on. Her black hair flowed behind her and her long legs raised clouds of dust. "I'm winning, Sun, I'm winning," she cried.

At last she reached the wall around the site and ran up to the first gang leader she could find. "Boat Gang," she panted. "Where will I find the Boat Gang?"

The man pointed towards the top of the huge pyramid. "Working up there today – rather them than me!" he grunted.

Nephoris groaned. The sun raced on and this time it was winning.

As Nephoris reached the foot of the pyramid she saw her father and the Boat Gang stomping down with heavy feet and grim faces. "Just in time," she muttered. "He looks in a rotten temper. If he'd opened his lunch pack and found a rat ... he might have eaten it in anger!"

Yenini glared at Nephoris. "What are you doing here? It's a dangerous place for a child. What is your mother thinking of? Wait until I get home."

"But I came to bring ..." Nephoris began.

Then there was a rumble and the men of the Boat Gang turned and looked up at the pyramid.

At the top of the pyramid ...

Chapter 4

Peril at the Pyramid

The Boat Gang had left their stone at the edge of the hole. The old wooden sledge grew hotter and drier in the midday sun. It creaked a little then it cracked.

The stone sank into the sledge and turned it to splinters and dust. Finally the stone began to slip. It slipped steadily into the hole that was waiting for it. The stone landed with a "whumph" and settled.

It was a perfect fit. It would stay there until long after the Boat Gang had finished their work, long after Amenemhat was buried inside, long after the grave robbers had stolen his wealth. It would stay there until the end of time.

Yenini raced up the steep ramp. He was the fastest of the Lisht men – smooth and swift as his daughter. Nephoris ran behind him. She caught him up at the top of the pyramid. She could see clear across Lisht, over her village and over the mud-brown flowing Nile.

Her father's redness shrank to a spot on each cheek. The rest of his face and body was pale and sweating. "What's wrong?" Nephoris asked. "It fell where it was supposed to. It saved you the work!"

"We'll never get it out," her father whispered as the men of the Boat Gang panted and wheezed up to their side.

"Why would you want to get it out?"
Nephoris asked, puzzled.

Yenini looked at her with haunted eyes.
"Because little Antef is underneath that
stone," he groaned. "Crushed."

"Like Oneney's beetles," Nephoris
said.

"We've killed the King's man. Now
the King will kill us," one of the workers
moaned.

"It was an accident," Nephoris said.

"We all hated him," Yenini sighed.
"No one will believe it was an accident."

"The King is coming this afternoon," a man said. "How do you think he will kill us?"

"Club us to death," someone suggested.

"Too quick and painless. Probably tie us to stakes in the desert and leave us to rot. Let the jackals eat us," another man argued.

They all began to wail and sob. "Throw us in a pit of poisoned snakes!" came one loud cry.

Suddenly a voice called out, louder than all the rest. "Stop it! Stop this pitiful noise!" Nephoris cried.

They stopped. They looked at the girl. "We're going to die-ie-ie!" an old man croaked.

"No you are not!" Nephoris said. "Get back to work. There is another stone waiting on the barge by the river. Get it on a sledge. Drag it up the pyramid. That's what you must be doing when the King arrives. Showing how hard you work for him – how much you worship him."

She waved a hand at the scene below. "Look! The Nile is flooding. Amenemhat has brought you life for another year. Let him see how much you love him. Get building!"

Yenini frowned. "He will want to see Antef driving us."

"And he will see Antef driving you," Nephoris promised.

"We can't pull him out from under the stone," a man argued.

"And if we did he'd be a bit ... flat," Yenini argued.

"Just *do* it!" Nephoris said. "I'll have Antef with you by the time you have the next stone at the foot of the pyramid."

The men looked bewildered but wandered back down the pyramid to obey her. Nephoris raced past them like a Nubian antelope and set off across the plain to Lisht.

Meanwhile...

King Amenemhat's boat drifted down the cool waters of the Nile and headed for Lisht ...

Chapter 5

The Dead Driver

King Amenemhat was carried in a shaded chair. That's the only way for a god to travel. When he reached the pyramid he opened the curtain and looked out. His face was as calm as the carved lions in the temple, but inside he was excited.

He watched the Boat Gang heaving on the ropes and singing a hymn. A hymn about their glorious King Amenemhat. His Majesty was pleased.

Walking alongside the Boat Gang was a little man with a perfumed wig and a plaited beard. Between the lines of the hymn the King could hear the little man shouting. It was not very pleasant.

"You are the biggest bunch of brainless beetles on this pyramid and all you can do is sing. You can't move one little stone and you think it's something to sing about?" he shouted in his voice that was thin as a Nile reed.

He raised the whip and tried to crack it. The end of the whip lashed back and caught him on the end of his nose.

"Don't laugh, you rabble of rats! Ouch! Ouch! Ouch! If one man laughs I will have him taken to the top of the pyramid and thrown off! Now h-e-a-v-e!"

King Amenemhat said to a servant, "Send Antef to me."

The servant hurried off and brought the little work-driver back. Antef held a hand to his injured nose and kept his eyes on the sizzling sand. All King Amenemhat could see was the dark wig and the plaited beard.

"Is the work going well, Antef?" the King asked.

"Very, very well. We shall be finished by harvest time. That Boat Gang from Lisht are wonderful."

"You shout at them a lot!"

"Ah, but only because we all love you so much, we want to do better than our best for you." Antef said humbly.

"Better than your best. Is that the best you can do?"

"It's better," Antef muttered. "May I get back to work now, your Majesty? They will be dropping that stone in place soon and I need to be there – we don't want any more accidents."

"Any more?" the King said. "Have there been any others?"

"No, your Majesty," Antef said, a little confused. "Just the odd crushed beetle. Nothing to worry about."

"Beetles?"

"Crushed."

The King leaned forward and peered at the work-driver. "Are you all right, Antef?" Antef pulled out a large rag and covered his face with it.

"Sorry, Majesty," he sniffled. "It was my favourite beetle."

The King blew out his cheeks. "Antef. I think the sun has boiled your brain. Go home and rest until you feel better. Make one of the Boat Gang the new work-driver."

"Yenini is very good, your majesty."

"Very well, Yenini is the new work-driver," he said and leaned back. "Servants! Take me back to the palace."

The covered chair was carried away.

If the King had looked back he'd have seen Antef tear off the itching wig and the scratchy beard then run up the pyramid to where Yenini was waiting.

Antef ran with the stride of a gazelle and the padding fell out of his robes. He no longer looked like a fat little work-driver. He looked more like a girl called Nephoris hugging her father Yenini.

Maybe it was …

Chapter 6
Beard Wigs and Earwigs

Nephoris walked home, arm in arm with her father, over the fields. She was carrying a purple robe, a perfumed wig and a beard wig. When they reached their village she handed them back to the artist Oneney and soon the fat statue of Antef was as good as new.

"I'm starving," Yenini said. "With all that bother at the pyramid I didn't even have time to eat my lunch."

"Your dinner is ready now," his wife said.

"No, it's a pity to waste good food," the man said. He pulled out his lunch packet and unwrapped it.

"Oh, Dad ..." Nephoris began.

Too late. Yenini was staring at a fat, dead rat. He gave a roar that could be heard at the top of the pyramid. He threw the rat through the open doorway into the long grass with curses that would have frightened the demons of the underworld.

He was roaring so loudly he didn't hear the little cry of fear from the grass where the rat had landed.

But little Pere's sharp ears heard it. He pulled himself onto his stumpy legs and wandered out of the house. "Rats," he muttered.

The stars were burning in the purple sky and a thin moon glittered on the inky Nile. Pere carefully pulled the grass apart and saw the man lying there. A short, fat, bald man. The dead rat was resting on his bald head where it had landed. He was quivering and too terrified to move it.

"Rats," Pere said.

"Oh, little boy, hush. Don't give me away. Spare me and I'll see the King gives you a purse of gold. But don't tell the men of Lisht I am here."

"Little man," Pere said.

"They tried to kill me, you know. Left me in a hole and went to eat their lunch. I was lucky. I caught one of the ropes on the sledge and pulled myself up. But I was a bit too heavy. I pulled the stone down. It fell just after I scrambled out. Oh, but I ran down the other side of the pyramid. They didn't see me. I bet they think they killed me!"

"Naughty man," Pere said. He picked up the dead rat and slapped Antef across the head with it. It fell to the ground.

"I've taken off my wig and beard so no one will know me," Antef babbled. "I've been hiding here all afternoon with the earwigs and spiders. When the moon sets I'll go down to the port and take the next boat out of Lisht. And I'll never come back. Never. They hate me."

Pere giggled.

"But I am so hungry," Antef groaned. "Can you give me something to eat, little boy? Please, please get me food – understand? Food. FOOD ..."

Pere looked hard at the man with a face-crumpling frown. Then he smiled his one-toothed smile. He reached on to the ground and said, "Food!"

He picked up the rat and used his fat little fist to stuff it into Antef's mouth.

Afterword

The Egyptians worked hard to build the massive stone pyramids for their kings. They worked in groups and had names like "The Boat Gang".

These men were paid in food, so building a pyramid wouldn't make them rich. But they were proud to do this service for the king who was their god. They believed their king-god made the River Nile flood. This flood each year made sure their crops grew.

While the fields were flooded they were free to work on the pyramids. It seems some of the king's officers treated the workers badly. They treated them like slaves and the proud peasants didn't like that. In 1170 B.C. the workers organized what was the first ever strike.

The workers marched together into the temple, refusing to work. They complained about a lack of food and drink, clothing and medicine. A scribe wrote down their complaints. Their message finally reached the Pharaoh, who arranged for the men to be paid with corn. Strikes of this kind happened again during the reign of Ramses III and even later pharaohs.

There were many accidents on these dangerous building sites. Some might have been deliberate. "Oooops! Sorry I dropped that 20 ton block on your head, boss!"

TERRY DEARY'S TALES

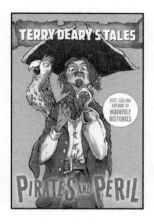